The Happy Egg

Story by RUTH KRAUSS

Pictures by CROCKETT JOHNSON

SCHOLASTIC BOOK SERVICES

NEW YORK · TORONTO · LONDON · AUCKLAND · SYDNEY · TOKYO

More books by Ruth Krauss and Crockett Johnson

Is This You?*

The Carrot Seed*

How to Make an Earthquake

*Available through Scholastic Book Services.

ISBN: 0-590-01623-7

23 22 21 20 19 18 17 16 15   01/8

Printed in the U.S.A.

07

The
Happy
Egg

There was a little little bird.

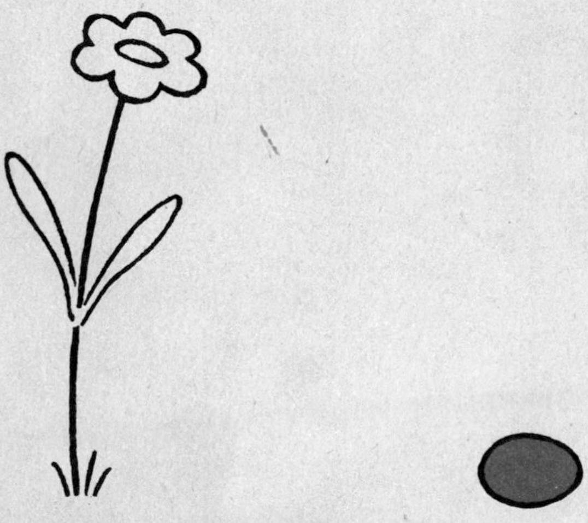

It was just born.
It still was an egg.

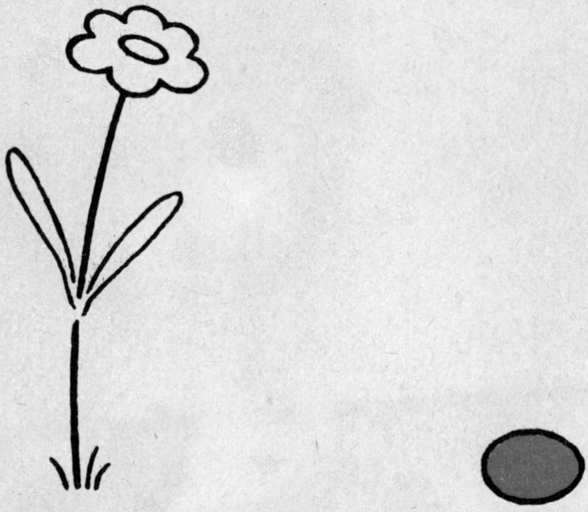

It couldn't walk.
It couldn't sing.
It couldn't fly.

It could just get sat on.

So it got sat on
and sat on

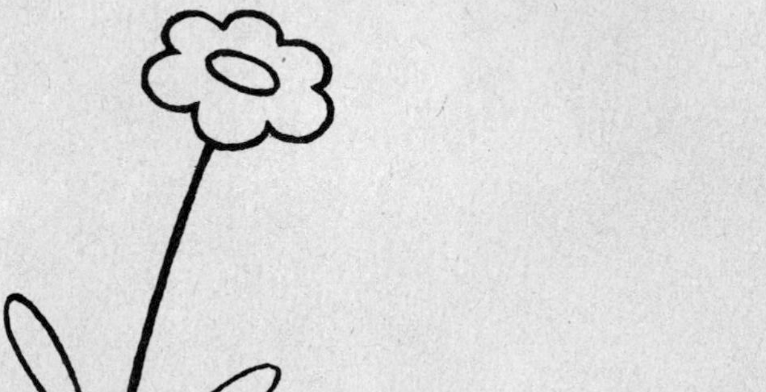

and sat on
and sat on

and sat on
and sat on
and sat on

and sat on.

And one day,

peep

POP! Out it came.

It could walk.

It could sing.

It could

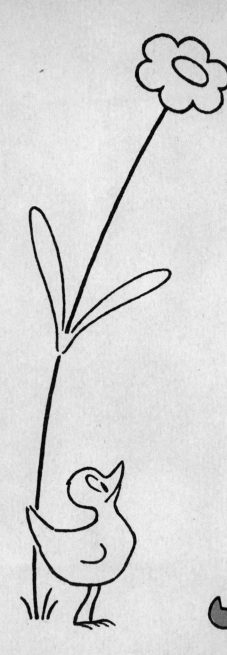

fly.

It could someday sit on
other happy eggs.